Woity's Adventure

An Unlikely Friendship

GISELA BENGFORT

Fulton Books, Inc.
Meadville, PA

Published by Fulton Books 2021

ISBN 978-1-63710-112-4 (paperback)
ISBN 978-1-63710-113-1 (digital)

Printed in the United States of America

Acknowledgment

To my best friend and the love of my life Joe Bengfort. Our children, Patrick, Lindsey, Selina, and Joseph.

To our grandchildren, Tim, Liam, Camryn, Vivienne, Elizabeth 'Lizzy,' and Josephine 'Jo.'

Special recognition is for our granddaughter Camryn, who lives close by and spent a lot of time with us, in her first five years. She inspired me to see the world through kids' eyes again; untainted, unfiltered, colorful, and without borders.

Legend: Rats have many enemies, and they use a special name for some of them including the following:

Humans: *smelly*
Birds of prey: *dark shadow*
Snakes: *sneaky one*
Animals with fur: *furry monster*

Chapter 1

Meet Wolfy

This is the story of Wolfy's adventure.

Don't be fooled by the name. Wolfy is a girl! To be precise, she is a young brown rat.

She'll take you on her daily journey. She will introduce you to all kinds of animals and will take you on endless adventures.

I am sure you will love her strong-willed attitude and character.

Q: Are you ready to hear her story?

Wolfy's family lives right beneath a big soccer field. To be precise, right underneath the goal that sat beside a beautiful redwood forest and neighborhood. The town's name is Mill Valley, a small town in California. They share the soccer field with geese also known as a gaggle of geese in a group.

She belongs to a large family of brown rats, also known as a pack of rats. Brown rats are nocturnal and belong to the species of Rattus.

She's the youngest of eight siblings. She has seven brothers. What might surprise you—they're all the same age. Wolfy was the last of the crop. She has to deal with seven brothers. Yup! Franky, Sunny, Jimmy, Silly, Porky, Charly, and Sparky.

Q: Can you see what all their names have in common?

The last letter in their names all end with a Y. Wolfy learned quickly to defend herself and to eat fast. She had to compete with seven hungry brothers. She learned to wolf down her food quicker than the others, so they all started to call her Wolfy. You surely understand when I tell you that there was a lot of bickering going on over food, Mom's attention, and not to mention the fight over toys.

Q: Can you guess what they eat?

The ones who live in the wild like her family love berries, vegetation, insects, twigs, nuts, small mammals, birds, and eggs. The rats who live close to cities eat pretty much everything.

Their home is nothing like yours, as I am sure you can imagine. Their homes have many entries and exits, not only because they live in big groups.

Q: Can you guess why?

Rats are small rodents who have many enemies and have to be able to get in and out quickly. Let me tell you a few of their enemies, also called predators.

Those on the ground level are cats, dogs, foxes, coyotes, snakes, and humans.

The other predators are in the air and are called large birds of prey. Those are hawks, falcon, and owls.

Q: Did you know the pack has different names for all of their enemies?

For example, cats, dogs, foxes, and coyotes are called *furry monsters.*

For snakes, it is *sneaky one.*

For humans, like you and me, it is *smelly.*

For birds of prey, it is *dark shadows.*

They have a lot of predators to worry about, but it doesn't stop them from enjoying their lives.

Q: Now that you know a bit more about their way of life, are you ready to learn more about Wolfy?

Wolfy's favorite activities are playing with friends and dinners with family. Sunflowers are her favorite flowers. She likes them because their flower head, also known as a carpel, follows the sun from morning to evening. The seeds in the middle of the Sunflower are delicious.

Wolfy is the smallest of all her siblings, but her size can be misleading. She's courageous, smart, spontaneous, and a kindhearted soul. She's proof that it doesn't take a large body to carry a big heart.

Her best friend is her brother Sparky. He always has great ideas. He loves to build different things from all the trash the *smelly* produce. He's kind of an inventor who wears his glasses proudly because it makes him look like a skilled engineer.

Wolfy dreams of flying away into the sky. She wonders where the sun is going down at dusk and coming up at dawn.

But her biggest wish is to own a dress. With only having brothers, there was just never a time to make a dress for a girl. Shhhh, it's her secret, and now yours too.

Q: Do you have a secret?

Chapter 2

Half a Tail Shorter

The sun just went down when Aunt Anny came storming into Wolfy's home. Crying, she reported that Uncle Rey didn't come home in the morning.

Apparently, he got caught by a *dark shadow* during the night.

This *dark shadow* was from a red-shouldered hawk family living in a large redwood tree right beside the soccer field.

"This has got to stop," said Wolfy's dad, Rolfy. "We're losing too many of our pack. We need to form a council. We need to come up with a new defense plan quickly."

Everyone agreed and word got around that the pack will meet on the next sunset in Wolfy's home.

Wolfy groomed herself and put her shirt and pants on so she could go outside and play with her friends.

Mom told her not to get dirty again. She wasn't sure Wolfy heard her because she was already out the door. She was a typical youngster, knew everything, and didn't like to listen so closely.

Q: Are you that way sometimes?

Wolfy loved to run! She was faster than most and was truly proud of it. She liked to challenge Sparky and win the race. It made her giggle.

Susy and Jerry were already waiting outside. They were siblings from a different rat pack. When she and Sparky arrived, they were asking, "Hey, what are we gonna do today?"

Wolfy suggested to explore the woods, and the others agreed happily.

What they didn't notice were two big eyes lurking behind a tree and watching them closely.

It was a *furry monster*, who followed them on its quiet paws.

Q: Oh no! Can you guess what that could be?

They all got excited when they found a shrub of wild berries, and all started to eat. The berries were juicy and fresh. Wolfy slobbered all over her shirt. Sparky was teasing her and called her a slobber puss.

Suddenly, the shrub moved, and a big cat came charging out, grabbing Wolfy. She tried to run as fast as she could the opposite way, but the cat caught her by her tail. She felt the pain in her back. She was hanging upside down with her head close to the ground.

The cat was running, and Wolfy got turned around. Just when she feared there was no escape, she got a hold of the cat's front paw.

She bit as hard as she could into it while hanging upside down. The cat screeched out and dropped Wolfy immediately.

She realized this was her only chance to get away. She wasn't looking where she was going or where her friends went. The most important thing on her mind was to make an impossible escape.

She saw a small hole by the foot of a tree. She took the chance and disappeared into it. She could feel the cat right behind her, but she made it and got away.

Her heart was pumping so hard that she was worried it would explode. She also felt the throbbing pain in her tail. She was bleeding. She almost fainted when she looked closer. Half of her tail was missing. She felt sick, forlorn, and whispered, "Mom!"

She whirled around when she heard some noise behind her.

"Is that you, Wolfy?" whispered a familiar voice. Out from the dark stepped Susy and Sparky. Her brothers' faces looked at her in total disbelief.

Wolfy was never so happy to see them. She told them what happened and how she managed to escape. They hugged each other and cried and talked over each other. When they calmed down, they quietly checked their surroundings.

"Pssst," said Wolfy, "let me check if the *furry monster* is gone." She tiptoed toward the exit, tilted her head, and looked outside.

She shrieked out holding her paw over her mouth not to be heard because looking right back at her were the cat's big scary eyes.

She gasped for air and stepped away from the entry, back into the dark. "Looks like we need to hide here till the cat gets bored and will look for her next meal somewhere else."

Wolfy's tail needed special attention, and she started to lick her wound. The bleeding stopped but not her pain.

Susy and Sparky both were still staring at Wolfy.

"What's the matter with you two? Have you never seen blood before?" said Wolfy

"No, silly," answered Susy, "I've seen blood before but never *one* rat who got away from *it*! You're amazing, Wolfy!"

Sparky agreed proudly and put his paw on her shoulder. It was his way to show Wolfy how proud he was of her.

They all cuddled close together. The warm comfort helped, and they fell asleep quickly. The adrenaline of this adventure exhausted them all, and they slept almost all night.

Wolfy's throbbing pain in her tail woke her up. She softly touched her companions.

"Let's check if the *furry monster* has lost her interest in us, and we can make a run for home. I am sure our family is worried about us."

She approached the entry slowly and held her breath while slowly sticking her head outside. Her eyes needed first to adjust to the outside. She could feel the cold air, but there was no *furry monster* smell.

"She's gone," said Wolfy.

Susy whispered to Wolfy, "Please lead us home."

"Yes," agreed Sparky.

All three took a big, deep breath and stepped outside. It was dark at first, and they were still spooked from the incident with the *furry monster*.

Wolfy grabbed both of their paws and started running into the dark. The silver moon up in the sky was bright and provided them some visibility. She held them tightly as if their life depended on it.

It was totally silent, and all they could hear was the beat of their own scared hearts. All three knew the dawn held a lot of danger for little rats like them.

When they reached Wolfy's home, all three were completely out of breath.

So was everyone else when they saw the trio storming in.

Wolfy's mom let out a loud cry of joy. Everyone turned their heads in disbelief toward the entry.

You can't imagine the joy and warm welcome they got. Hundreds of questions were asked at once. There was total chaos. They built a circle around Wolfy, and Jerry stepped forward looking spooked at Wolfy like she was a ghost.

His mouth was opening and closing, without making a sound. After he found his composure again, he said in a high-pitched voice, "You're ALIVE!"

Then he tried in a deeper voice again, "YOU ARE ALIVE? How can that be? I saw the *furry monster* carry you away! No one ever gets back from that! We ALL know that!"

Then Susy stepped forward. "She bit the *furry monster*! She bit *it*, and it screamed and dropped her!"

Sparky, still a bit pale and out of breath from running, nodded his head up and down quickly, "YES, Wolfy, you're my HERO!"

All of them gazed over at Wolfy with admiration and amazement.

They started chanting, "WOLFY, WOLFY, WOLFY!"

Wolfy was standing on the small entry rug when, suddenly, everyone picked up the rug and threw her up in the air. They experienced an overwhelming joy of victory. Wolfy showed them that there's hope, and you can win if you give it your all and never give up!

Wolfy's face also showed some pain.

Mom stepped forward and shouted. "STOP, STOP! Can't you see Wolfy is injured?" They put the rug down carefully.

Wolfy didn't feel much like a hero. She felt more like a young rat girl, tired and hurt.

Mom went to get some herbs for her injury. She put chamomile leaves on the end of Wolfy's tail to prevent infection and put a couple of arnica leaves in her mouth to chew on. Arnica is known for reducing bruises and swelling.

Mom put her down to bed and had everyone go home so their new little hero could rest and sleep.

That was the night Wolfy became their *hero*!

The rest of the night was filled with dreams—and nightmares.

Remember, they go to bed when you get up and vice versa.

Wolfy was allowed to sleep with Mom and Dad to feel safe. Sparky was lying in his bed with his arms behind his head thinking of Wolfy!

My sister the hero, he proudly thought about his little sister when he fell asleep.

Q: Do you have nightmares sometimes? What do you do to feel safer?

The next morning Susy and Jerry watched the sunrise together, talking about every detail of the night before.

Their recollection of the night gotten bigger and bigger and *bigger* in their little heads.

Chapter 3

Wolfy Meets Her Destiny

The next few nights were not as much of an adventure as they were reflections of the past days. The whole pack mourned Rey's passing by the *dark shadow*. They also celebrated Wolfy's survival by biting the *furry monster*.

It was a bittersweet moment realizing that sometimes you win and sometimes you lose.

Q: Have you ever lost someone you loved?

Wolfy asked Mom if she could visit Aunt Anny to provide her some comfort. Mom was pleased to hear that but urged Wolfy not to go above the surface.

It was possible to reach her aunt's home through the burrows without going to the surface, and it was much safer for a rat.

Wolfy agreed, even though she loved the surface more than staying down in the burrows. There was so much more excitement out there.

She helped Aunt Anny to sort out some stuff, and they cooked together. She made her aunt smile when she said, "Your cakes are just the best!"

They talked about Rey and the many memories they made over the years together. They had more tears and laughter. When the night turned into dawn, also called twilight because of the transition, Wolfy gave Aunt Anny a big hug and left for home.

Halfway home, Wolfy forgot her promise to stay in the tunnel and left through an exit.

She surfaced into a beautiful vegetable yard and decided to nip on some tasty strawberries. There was some metal chicken wire over the berries to protect them from birds.

She felt very safe.

Suddenly, a *dark shadow* was over her, hitting the mesh really hard with his claws, trying to catch her. The talon ripped her furry skin and made her screech a bit.

The bird couldn't get a grip on Wolfy because of the chicken wire. She shivered from the close call.

The *dark shadow* said, "Don't worry, rat, I will get you one of these days. Too bad I saw the chicken wire too late. That won't happen again."

Chills went up and down from her head to her tiny toes. When Wolfy figured out she was out of reach and safe, she got her confidence back. She looked up to the bird with her arms on her waist.

"My name is Wolfy, and I fought off a *furry monster.* I am sure I can fight you off too."

The bird snickered and looked through its claws down through the chicken wire at Wolfy. "Oh, I've heard of you! Not that it matters to you, but my name is Fate, and I will be your destiny. I will be the destiny of your whole PACK!"

There was that chill again, knowing the *dark shadow* might be right. Regardless, Wolfy didn't want Fate to know of her fear and she laughed, maybe a bit too loud, but she stood tall.

"We will see whose destiny will be whose," said Wolfy.

She exited quickly down the tunnel and ran home. She didn't want to give Fate another chance to scare her.

Now what! She couldn't tell Mom. She promised she would stay in the tunnel, and she didn't.

That morning, Wolfy was very quiet at the table and remembered what Fate said. It frighted her, and she couldn't wait to tell Sparky, her friend and confidant, about it.

All her siblings were talking, laughing, and telling their night adventures; one of Wolfy's favorite activities.

Dad looked suspiciously over at Wolfy. "What went on with your night, Wolfy?" he asked. "Why are you so quiet like a mouse?"

That made everyone giggle since they're rats, not mice.

She blushed immediately and stuttered, "I...spent... *all*...night...with Aunt Anny. *Nothing* happened."

She felt very bad lying about it and took a big bite so she couldn't talk further.

Her dad was giving her a long look. He saw the deep cut on her neck and knew she wasn't telling the whole truth, but he let her get away with it. He loved Wolfy's free spirit and was proud of her.

Q: Do you know that feeling, blushing because you didn't tell the whole truth?

She went early to bed and thought about her encounter with Fate. Chills still ran through her just thinking about it. She fell into a restless sleep with her blanket over her head.

Q: Can you guess why?

Chapter 4

A Call for Help

Wolfy woke up just before daybreak when it was still dark, and some stars could be seen. She heard a desperate cry.

"Help, help, please somebody help me!"

She checked on her siblings who were all deep asleep. She tiptoed out of the bedroom and went carefully toward the closest exit.

She spied through the hole and saw the blanket of stars and a sliver of the moon. Her eyes needed to adjust to the outside light. She looked around and couldn't see anyone that needed help. Just when she was turning around to go back down, she heard it again.

"Help, please, help me!" This time, she looked from where the voice came. She spotted something wiggling in the soccer net.

Carefully, she approached the site. She recognized a *dark shadow* tangled in the net of the soccer goal, hopelessly wiggling to free itself. The more the bird wiggled, the more it got entangled. When Wolfy was closer, and her eyes adjusted to the darkness, she recognized who it was. It was Fate! Fate saw Wolfy and pleaded for help.

"Please, help me! My wings are badly tangled in the net. I am stuck! I can't get out without your help!"

"Helping *you?*" spit Wolfy. "*You?* What's with 'you're my destiny' and you will eat me? Do I look that dumb to you? Give me one reason why I should free you? So you could eat me and my family?"

Fate struggled and tried not to show the sheer fear in her eyes. She might be eaten by a hungry creature like a cat or a fox. She couldn't defend herself and would be left to their mercy.

"What would you ask of me in order for you to help me?" Fate asked.

"Look at me," said Wolfy. "I am tiny! Any promise you would give to me would be useless once you're free. I would be at your mercy as you are at mine right now. Besides, I'm not sure that I could even free you."

Fate's wings were hurting, and her voice broke a bit.

"I would promise never to eat you or your family. I would leave this place and fly far away. Please help me! I know it is hard to trust me after all. I swear by the beat of my heart to never hurt you! *Ever!*"

Fate started quietly crying. For the first time, Wolfy felt deeply sorry for her. She went a bit closer to look at the mesh of the net and what it would take to free her.

"You've got to understand, Fate, my family wouldn't understand why I would help you. We have so many enemies. We're so tiny and helpless. We don't have friends in higher places like you."

Fate looked at Wolfy. "Do you see any friends in high places helping me right now? My family couldn't help with the net. They tried but then left when there was no chance to free me. Believe me, they would have helped but simply couldn't. You're the only one who can help me now."

So many things went through Wolfy's little head that she got dizzy. She sat down and held her head with her paws. She was thinking.

Fate's voice got weaker and the pain bigger.

She said, "I understand your dilemma. I am sorry to put you into this position. I would have doubts helping you if I were in your shoes. I plea for mercy. I appeal to your tiny heart. Please take a leap of faith and trust me. Maybe we could become friends!"

Wolfy's head tilted toward Fate. "Friends you say. How could that be? I am on your food list, and you're my archenemy. How in the world could we be friends?"

Fate replied, "We're talking together are we not?"

"Yes," Wolfy said, forlorn.

Fate got quiet and was just hanging there. Both got quiet for a while. After a long silence, Wolfy asked worriedly, "Are you still alive Fate?" No answer. She jumped up to her feet. She was worried Fate might be dead.

"Fate!" whispered Wolfy, but this time louder.

"Oh, you start to care now?" asked Fate. "Will you help me, Wolfy, please? I will dedicate the rest of my life to yours, please!"

Wolfy said, "Of course I care, Fate, I don't like seeing you in such pain. I appreciate you walking in my shoes to understand my dilemma."

Suddenly, Wolfy knew what to do. Just the thought Fate could die right before her eyes troubled her deeply.

That's not who she was or wanted to become. Just because she was tiny didn't determine the size of her heart.

Q: What would you do, and why?

Wolfy started climbing up the mesh toward Fate. "I guess your help comes from below, and don't you forget that. If you break your promise and you eat me afterward, I hope you will choke."

Fate's eyes were glued on Wolfy while she started chewing through the rope of the soccer net.

When Fate's feather and Wolfy's fur touched they both felt electricity going through their bodies. After she took a break for a moment, she looked at Fate and asked how she was doing.

Fate said quietly but with a swing of hope in her voice, "Never been better, my friend!"

Wolfy smiled, wondering herself if they really could be friends.

She started chewing again. Finally, one wing came free. One more to go. Fate hung upside down and closed her eyes. The pain grew stronger hanging only on one wing.

Wolfy told Fate during one of her short breaks about one of her dreams: flying high in the sky toward the sun.

Then the last rope was chewed through and Fate fell to the ground. She was lying lifeless on the soccer field. Very slow and carefully, Fate stood up and looked up to Wolfy who was still holding on to the net. Wolfy started to have a strange feeling in her belly.

Wolfy said hastily, "Now what?"

Fate stretched her wings and legs and said, "All great. Nothing broken, but now looking at you, I realize how hungry I am."

Wolfy swallowed hard! Fate took a step closer to Wolfy.

Wolfy was just about to remind Fate of her pledge when Fate started to laugh.

"Just kidding, my friend, just kidding."

They both laughed, but Fate definitely louder and harder than Wolfy. Fate took a step closer to Wolfy and tilted her head, so their eyes were locked with each other.

They both felt that this moment changed them forever.

"Thank you from the bottom of my heart for trusting me," said Fate. She stood right beneath Wolfy nudging her. "Now jump on my back." Wolfy slowly glided down from the net onto Fate's back. Wow, Fate felt so warm and cozy.

Fate said, "Hold on, my friend. Let's make one of your dreams come true!"

Wolfy positioned herself and got a good grip on Fate's back feathers. Fate swung her wings and up they went. She heard *swoosh, swoosh*, the sound of the wings while they gained height.

Wolfy felt the cool air going through her fur. It took her breath away, but it was the view that left her breathless. She could still see the moon on one side and the sun coming up on the other side. It was amazing! Everything seemed so small beneath them, and at the same time, she has never seen that far ahead.

Wolfy asked, "What's that blue glaring thing over there, Fate?"

"Oh, that's the Richardson Bay. It's ocean water," said Fate.

"Wow!" Wolfy was speechless!

They flew for a while over the bay. Fate made a big circle back to the soccer field toward both of their homes.

One high up, and the other underground. One had feathers, the other had fur. One could fly, the other run. One is diurnal and awake during the day, and the other is nocturnal and awake at night. A bit like the sun and the moon.

Could this be the beginning of something unthinkable? Like a friendship?

Q: Do you have a friend who's different from you?

Wolfy leaned on Fate, and they hugged each other. Fate bent down.

"You really do smell fantastic," said Fate. And this time, both laughed together.

"When do I see you again?" Wolfy asked.

Fate replied, "I promised to leave home and fly far away! I pledged not to harm you or any of your family members, and I will keep my promise."

Wolfy asked, "Yes, but how can we be friends if we part now?"

That of course was a good question.

"My family will probably honor your life for saving mine," said Fate. "But I'm not sure if that would include your family."

Wolfy hadn't even thought about the consequences this friendship would have on her family. They would be furious at her for saving a *dark shadow*; one of the biggest enemies a rat pack could have.

They were sitting beside each other, brainstorming how to solve this dilemma.

Fate said, "Okay, here's the thing, let's talk with our families. Can't be that bad, right?"

"Right," Wolfy said hesitantly.

Suddenly, both lost confidence and hope, not sure that their families would understand this at all. They both felt so worried and sad. How could something feel so good yet be so bad for someone else?

"How will we stay in touch?" asked Wolfy.

Fate said, "Just call me. I will hear you and definitely see you!"

Wolfy touched Fate's wings amiably and took off toward home. She was tired but felt a new heartbeat in her chest.

Q: Do you know why?

Wolfy sneaked into her bedroom and quietly lay down. She couldn't fall back asleep. She met an unlikely friend, and it felt so good, and it was so different than anything she ever encountered in her whole life. The excitement was overwhelming!

Chapter 5

Stepping Up

Wolfy got back up and tiptoed over to Sparky's bed. She gently woke him up by touching his shoulder. He jumped up while still half asleep.

"Whaaaat?" he asked, a bit worried. "What's with the early wake-up call, sis?"

She crawled under his blanket and put her paw to her lips signaling to be quiet.

"I freed a *dark shadow* from the soccer net before sunrise," said Wolfy. "Her name is Fate. She then took me for a flight, and I saw the ocean. We're friends now!"

She rattled it all out really quickly to get it off her chest. Her brother looked in total disbelief to Wolfy.

"Go back to sleep, sis," said Sparky. "You just dreamt this. Free a *dark shadow*? Who in their right mind would do something so ridiculous?" He shook his head signaling, "No, no." Sparky lay back down and turned to the side hoping to catch some more sleep.

Wolfy exclaimed, "It's true. I did it!"

Sparky got up in slow motion and looked at Wolfy as though he was seeing her for the very first time in his life.

"You can't tell anybody about this, sis! No one will understand!" Sparky shook her shoulders even harder.

"No, Sparky, I have every intention to tell everyone about it. Fate and I are friends now."

"FRIENDS! Do you hear yourself, sis? You can't be friends with your enemy!" Sparky said.

He lost his patience. He was frustrated with his sister's ignorance. His paws were still on her shoulder, and he pushed her harder than he intended to and Wolfy fell backward.

She looked with tears in her eyes at Sparky. She dusted off her pants while she got up. Her gaze was glued on her brother.

Wolfy said, "Of all the friends in the world, I thought you would understand. I thought you would support me."

She turned and walked away. She tried to hold the tears of disappointment back that were rolling down her face.

Sparky ran guiltily behind her and said, "Stop, Wolfy!"

Then out of nowhere, their Dad was standing in their room. He was looking from one to another.

"Trouble in paradise?" he asked. "At the crack of dawn?"

They both folded their paws in front of them and kept totally silent. Dad looked worriedly at Wolfy when he saw the tears rolling down her face.

"What happened?" he asked. He looked questionably over to Sparky.

Sparky said, "I didn't do anything, Dad! Ask your daughter," he said defensively.

"Wolfy? I am listening," said Dad.

She ran toward her dad and wrapped her paws around him and said, "I saved a *dark shadow*. Her name is Fate. I saved her. Then we flew together over the bay. We're friends now!"

Her dad was very quiet for a moment then said, "Stay in your room, both of you. I am very disappointed in your behavior. We'll talk about it later."

His face was in deep thought. He turned around and left without another word. Wolfy sat on her bed and cried quietly. Sparky was angry at Wolfy. They both waited for hours with no breakfast, no lunch, and no sign from anyone. First, they started to fight over who put whom into this situation.

Sparky exclaimed, "This is all on you, sis!"

Wolfy looked forlorn at Sparky. After pouting for a while, they both felt sorry.

They gazed at each other and said, "I am sorry," at the same moment.

Q: Do you fight with your siblings or your friends sometimes? Are you the one starting or stopping the argument?

Sparky put his paw around Wolfy's shoulder and said, "I still think you're as crazy as a nut, but you're my little nut."

They both laughed, and then Dad entered the room. He told them to come in the living room to talk.

For rats, the living room is where all tunnels come together into a big space of shelter.

They both were expecting to have a talk with Dad, Mom, and their siblings.

When they stepped into the room, their eyes got big, and they saw that the whole village pack was present!

Dad started to address everyone and said, "Thank you, everyone, for coming to this meeting on such short notice. I am calling this meeting to avoid gossip and rumors. We're here to understand special circumstances that life can present, to exercise tolerance toward different opinions, and to show some compassion for helping someone in distress. Wolfy, my daughter, will tell all of you what happened to her in the dawn of the day. Don't interrupt her till she's finished telling the whole story. I don't know the whole story either, so I will learn with you about what happened."

Q: Did you ever have to talk to a whole classroom or family? Do you remember the rush you felt through your whole body?

Wolfy was stunned, scared, and terrified to step in front of everybody to tell her story. All eyes were on her. She took a deep breath and looked at her dad.

Wolfy started, "First of all, I would like to apologize to my family if I scared you or disappointed you in any way. It was not my intention at all."

Her trembling voice started to be steadier as she began to tell her whole story from the beginning to the end. There were many times during telling the story that others would say "OH NO!" and "WHAT?" or "TRAITOR!" then "UNBELIEVABLE!" and so on. Every time someone said something, they got a silent gaze from Rolfy, Wolfy's dad.

Wolfy ended with the part where she flew with Fate and that they were friends now. The room fell totally silent.

Wolfy's dad used this moment to talk. "Now, before you are all accusative toward Wolfy, I would like to tell you a story of my own! My story!"

Chapter 6

Dad's Story

Wolfy's dad started, "You all know me as Rolfy. I am Wolfy's dad, but this is not the place I grew up. This is the place I chose to raise my family where I helped to create a strong community. Many years ago, when I was Wolfy's age, we lived far, far away from here. It was a beautiful place called Switzerland. The food, the weather, and the language were very different from here, but the hope of a good life wasn't any different from what I encountered here. We are the same after all. We lived in a big pack and had plenty of food. We lived on a farm in the mountains and had daily feasts and parties. Life was great!"

Q: Have you and your family moved away before?

Rolfy continued, "One day, the *smelly* ones came and threw lots of 'new food' down to our tunnels. Many of the rats ate it and shortly after got very sick and died. My mother and I were the sole survivors of the whole pack."

"We left our home that same night. Our hearts were broken, and we didn't know what the future might bring. Looking back, I know my mom gave up everything for a better future for me. We left the only place we ever knew and called home. The road we took was dangerous. The entire journey was on the surface, and we didn't have much protection. We met plenty of rats along our journey. Some were nice and shared the little they had with us. Others were territorial, mean, and chased us away.

"One day, we entered a big warehouse that someone had mentioned to Mom. We were hiding in a big container that had cheese in it. Little did we know that the next morning, big trucks would come, loaded us up, and took us away. They brought the container where we were hiding onto a train and shipped us away. We got loaded into a big metal *dark shadow*, and we flew over the big Atlantic Ocean. That's how my mom and I came to the United States of America, precisely to the City of San Francisco.

"We arrived on a pier with the truckload of cheese and were dropped off in a warehouse. We found some work by a local wealthy rat pack in the city. I was ordered to gather food and my mom to prepare it. My mom was a true chef. She had incredible knowledge of herbs and how to use them to make food taste great."

Q: Do you know what herbs are?

Some herbs look like vegetables and some like flowers some like a tree or a root, but all have a healing purpose.

Rolfy continued, "Now, this warehouse was actually quite dangerous. The *smelly* had several *furry monsters* in this warehouse, and they were constantly hunting us.

"We had a little spare room that we shared with many others. Many were from different countries and spoke different languages. Their reasons for leaving their homes were similar to ours in some cases and different in others, but we all had one common dream, survive and make a better life for ourselves and our families. We ate the leftovers that the wealthy rats gave us, but most of the time, I fell asleep hungry.

"Mom's name was Marianne, and she always told me that her name had the meaning of 'liberty.' She never lost hope, bless her heart."

Everyone was glued to Rolfy's story, and they sat quietly to hear every word. At times when the story got intense, you could hear a sharp intake of a gasp and other times a relieved exhale.

"My mom never complained," Rolfy continued. "On the contrary! She encouraged me to be proud of where I came from and who I was. She'd say, 'Remember your family, Rolfy. Have hope, Rolfy,' as she put some of her spare food onto my plate. She always smiled and mentioned that I was still growing and needed it more than she.

"She'd say, 'One day, little Rolfy, we will have a better life.' That day came when the *smelly* ones arrived. They put many 'food boxes' on the ground. The smell was so tempting. We saw many rats going into the boxes who couldn't resist the smell, but none came back out.

"My Mom had that awful memory from what happened in Switzerland. Knowing that this smell was bad and would kill us all, she screeched from the top of her lungs at all of them. 'Don't eat that! It will hurt your belly, and you will feel very sick, and then you will die. I've seen this before! Listen to me!'

"Her boss didn't believe her. As a matter of fact, many didn't believe her and went inside the box and ate it. Her boss pushed her away and said, 'Go back to work. You're just jealous of my wealth and that the *smelly* love us so much that they're providing food for my pack.'

"Of course, those who ate that food didn't make it. The rest of us decided to move away from the city. We climbed up into a food delivery bus. Every day we had seen those buses come into the warehouse to pick up goods. We didn't know where this would lead us, but any place was better than this one.

"My mom told me, 'Have hope, Rolfy, and life will be better. This is just a new adventure, Rolfy. Liberty is coming!' The bus drove over a big red bridge called Golden Gate Bridge into this town where we are today, Mill Valley. We found this new place, but we couldn't have done it without the help of many others. We didn't know each other, but we took a leap of fate.

"Trust is one of the most important ingredients in a friendship. It takes courage to trust someone new. You have to invest time for a friendship to grow, and it only takes a split second to lose that established trust."

Q: Have you ever disappointed someone you care about? The words "I am sorry" can be very powerful and meaningful.

Rolfy continued, "It demands hard work and courage to create a new life. It also takes some luck along your way.

"Together, we became a big successful pack. It has grown into something more than me and my mom could have ever dreamed of. All because the rat pack we met here in Mill Valley, your ancestors, trusted us and gave us a chance."

Rolfy looked sincerely to the rat pack and said, "I am entirely grateful for your friendship. Please show some of that trust and friendship to my daughter. Should she have come to us and ask for help? Yes, but sometimes there's not enough time to do so, and you have to follow your heart. You have to have the courage to do the unthinkable and make it happen. All I am asking from you is to do the same."

Rolfy bent over and took a preserved edelweiss out of his pocket. Proudly, he held it over his head and let out a little yodel.

After that, he said, "I too needed a reminder to be proud of my heritage. My daughter's courage is the blend of two beautiful countries. I am lucky to have her. My mom's strong will and spirit lives in my daughter. I am proud of my heritage because that's who I am, and I see it in Wolfy."

He stopped talking, and it was totally silent. No one said a word, but you could see they were all in deep thought.

The silence broke when Sparky asked, "Am I a Swiss too, Dad?"

"Yes, son, you're the best of both! You're an immigrant who is part of building this beautiful country," Rolfy replied.

Everyone had questions at once.

"Do you miss Switzerland?"

"Yes, very much," Rolfy replied. "I miss the smell of fresh-cut grass and dried hay, and I miss the sound of cowbells as they grazed on the hills and the sound of the mountain streams rushing down. The yodeling during our gatherings, and of course, I miss the view of the striking mountain ranges themselves."

"Which is your favorite place now?"

"Home," Rolfy answered.

After Rolfy answered many questions, they all realized that they have forgotten Wolfy.

Someone asked, "What now, Wolfy? What are you gonna do about *your* new friend?"

"She could be your friend too," Wolfy said.

"Why did you help one of our biggest enemies?" asked another.

Wolfy said, "Fate needed help, and I am not heartless, and I would do it again."

"But she could have killed you! Weren't you afraid?" asked someone.

Wolfy said, "Yes, but I took that leap of faith, and now, I have a new friend. Also, Fate promised not to eat any of my family," continued Wolfy, gesturing with her paws toward all of them.

"We'll see about that, right?" all said aloud.

And someone shouted, "Yeah, we saw what they did to Rey!"

Wolfy's face turned sad, and she shrugged her shoulders and said, "I don't know about that. I haven't had a chance to talk to Fate and what the outcome of her family discussion will be."

Rolfy took a step forward and stood beside Wolfy. He put his arm on her shoulder and looked at the others and said, "She has answered all that she knows. Let's all just stay careful of the *dark shadow* until we know more about it."

Dad looked at Wolfy. She looked tired, but probably, she was even hungrier than tired. He said, "Someone had a long night and an even longer day. We all could use a good day of sleep. Thanks, my dear friends, for coming and for your ongoing support and friendship."

He took his preserved edelweiss and gave it to Wolfy. "It's yours now, and you shall be the keeper of our heritage."

She held it with both paws and walked very carefully and let out a little yodel. It sounded funny, and everyone got a good laugh out of it while leaving.

Mom had the table ready, and all sat down. This time, Wolfy wasn't the only one wolfing down her food. Sparky used both paws and stuffed himself silly.

Mom wanted to scold him, but Dad held her paw and shook his head and said, "Not tonight, my love."

Then they kissed.

The kids said simultaneously, "Eeeewwwww!" with their full mouths, and they all giggled.

Q: Do you do that too?

Chapter 7

Fate Tells Her Story

Fate was really tired; in fact, she was exhausted. She flew up to her home finding her brother Flo there.

"Wow, *you*! Didn't expect to see you ever again. How did you get out of that net?"

She looked proud at him. "Well, I've got friends in low places, and they come through when needed."

"Whaaaat!" Flo said, "Fate, that's not fair. I wanted to help you. You know I tried!"

Fate said, "Yes, you did, but then you just left me!"

"There was nothing more I could have done!" Flo protested. "Besides, why should we argue? You're here! That's all that matters."

He wrapped his wings around Fate and gave her a hug. "It's great to have you back, sister. You know Mom was devastated to leave you behind like that."

The sky threw a dark shadow when Fate's parents flew into the nest. Her mom was beside herself with joy. She kept hugging Fate and jumped up and down screeching very loud. "She's saved, she's saved. She's alive, she's alive," Fate's mom cried.

Her dad rolled his eyes at his wife Fancy. "Calm down, love," he chuckled. He stepped toward Fate and gave her a heartfelt hug. "Welcome back, girl. You're a sight for sore eyes. Don't mind Mom, you know her."

Flo asked, "So tell us for real how in the world you got out of this situation."

Fate groomed her feathers carefully pretending to be busy and said, "A rat saved me! Her name is Wolfy!"

Her brother rolled over on his back laughing so hard. "Stop, stop, you're killing me. Wolfy the rat saved my sister?" He was holding his belly from shaking so hard. "My sister got saved by a rat. Guess you ate her afterward, right?" He kept laughing and making fun of Fate. "Not everyone gets saved by their favorite dinner!" Flo laughed even harder.

"I didn't eat her," said Fate, frustrated, and pushed Flo to the ground. "She's my friend now!"

Her brother got back on his legs, shaking his feathers strongly.

"That's not funny, Fate! That will *never* work, and you know it!" He leaned very close to Fate and locked eyes with her. "This will *never* work," he said even louder.

Fate moved agitated away from him. She stood tall and gazed over at Flo and her parents. They looked speechless at this unfolding story and scene.

Fate said, "I promised her that I would never harm her or any of her family. I committed to leave if I can't uphold my promise. I told her that I would ask the same of you all as a token of gratitude for saving me."

"You must be out of your mind making such promises to our favorite food supply!" Flo said, looking daringly at his sister.

He screeched very loud to show his disapproval and stamped hard with his claws on the branch. Her Mom looked terrified around her and was absent for words.

Fate's dad, Fer, straightened his posture and shook his feathers looking sternly at Fate and said, "We're truly grateful to your friend for saving you. I am sure we all can agree to spare her life."

"What about her whole pack?" Fate asked her dad.

He shook his head and said, "This is the most commitment I am willing to make, but nothing more. This is our livelihood we're talking about, Fate. We work hard daily to keep our territory and food supply going. You know how difficult and dangerous this is. The ravens, crows, hawks, and owls are challenging us daily. Many times, we had to give up our food to them in order to survive. You know how they chase us! We can't give up our home, Fate. Not even for *you!*"

Her mom, Fancy, nodded her head up and down approving of what Dad said.

Q: Can you see what all of the hawks' names have in common?

All their names start with an F!

"You know very well the rule of the sky, Fate," Mom said.

Fate looked from one family member to the next stopping at Dad and said, "Well, I will point out Wolfy to all of you expecting you will honor my vow and spare her. I will leave this home, my only home, and go away."

"Why?" asked her mom. "Why would you give up everything you love. They're just rats, and you eat rats!"

Fate looked mercifully at her whole family. Tears were rolling out of her huge dark eyes as she tilted her head downwards so they couldn't see her sadness.

"I know, Mom, this is a huge sacrifice. Without the existence of that rat…which, by the way, has a name… Wolfy…without Wolfy, there would be no sacrifice necessary."

Q: Do you know why?

"Because without her, there would be no Fate. I owe my life and everything I am to her."

She looked at her parents and her brother and looked into their gloomy faces. She knew they said the truth about their daily fight for survival. She knew they were loyal and loved her. She knew they wouldn't want her to leave. She also knew how hard it would be for her to leave all this behind. She knew how much she would miss everyone and everything, but she also knew that without Wolfy, there would be no Fate.

Promises are to keep, not to break.

She felt anxiety sneaking up! What now? She needed to talk to Wolfy. Inform her of her family's final decision. They would spare her life, but not the rest of the pack.

She turned her head toward them. They all were sitting beside each other looking so trist and sorrowful.

"I will be back later." And she flew off.

Q: What do you think Wolfy's brother and Fate's brother have in common?

Yes, both were not happy with their sisters' choice of friends first.

Chapter 8

Important Decisions

Fate didn't fly far away from home before she stopped and perched on a branch. She was in a grave mood and pensive.

What to do now?

While sitting up there, she was naturally scanning the grounds below her. The steady wind stopped, and a slow rain set in. It was more like misting. It felt like the sky was crying with her, picking up on her current sad mood.

Suddenly, she saw a rat running from one shrub to the next. She recognized that it wasn't Wolfy. Not far away from the rat, she saw a *sneaky one* picking up the rat's scent.

The *sneaky one* was turning and slithering toward the rat. The rat stopped and started eating some nuts from the shrub. The rat was totally unaware and ignorant of the danger close by. Out of nowhere, Wolfy joined the rat. It looked like they knew each other, and they were having a good time nudging each other playfully away from the nuts. Both shrieked with laughter.

Fate was a bit jealous. She didn't have anyone to have that kind of a friendship, with that comfort of belonging together.

Q: Do you have a friend like that?

The *sneaky one* was closing in on the two rats, ready to strike and have herself a little snack.

Fate thought for a split moment that this could be the solution to her dilemma. If the snake would eat Wolfy, she would be free of her promise. She could stay, and all her problems would be solved. No Wolfy! No broken vows! She could live happily ever after. Or could she?

She would have to live with the knowledge that she could have prevented this and save Wolfy's life.

Q: What would you do in her situation? Could you live with that?

Just when the *sneaky one* coiled up to strike Wolfy and the other rat, Fate knew what to do.

Fate dived down from the sky. Her wings were tucked and folded backward. She came down fast and grabbed the snake.

At the same time, her brother Flo dived down and grabbed the other rat!

Fate held the snake tight with her claws, and Flo did the same with the rat.

Wolfy shrieked out loud, "Sparky!" turning totally pale.

Fate snapped at Flo, "Release the rat, brother!"

"Why, is this your new friend Wolfy?" Flo replied.

Sparky was snatched tight in Flo's claws and couldn't move. He was so traumatized that he totally lost his voice. Flo held him so tight that he had a hard time to breath.

Wolfy got her courage back, stepped forward, and shouted, "No! This is my brother Sparky! I am Wolfy!"

Flo looked over at Fate, and in a snarky tone said, "In that case, we're all good. You got the snake, and I got Sparky. Fair and square, sister. I am not eating your friend like we all agreed."

Flo bent down to Wolfy, looking her up and down, then straight into her eyes and said, "Don't worry, rat, I'm just imprinting your face. We don't want to make a mistake and eat my sister's new pet."

Wolfy pleaded with Flo and cried, "Please, have mercy on my brother. I love him dearly!"

Flo shook his head, "Sorry, can't do it. Flo is hungry. Flo has to eat. It's that simple." He looked through his talons at a terrified Sparky.

Fate knew her brother well and could see the warning sign. Flo always means what he said. No exceptions!

Fate looked pleadingly at her brother and displayed her most charming self. Leaning toward him in a friendly gesture.

"Can we make a deal, brother?" Fate asked.

"What would that be?" replied Flo.

"It's more like a trade…the rat for my snake?" offered Fate.

He looked from the rat to the snake and back to the rat. Measuring who would provide more food to him.

"Okay, sister, deal! Be aware that this is the first and last time that I agree to such a deal. No more favors! Do you understand this?" Flo asked. He gazed over at Fate and his look sent chills through her veins.

Fate nodded her head in agreement. She let go of the snake, and Flo let go of Sparky. Flo grabbed the snake and flew away right over Wolfy. Wolfy was startled and ducked down.

"Please excuse my brother," said Fate, "he can be such a jerk."

Q: Have you ever done a trade like that or have you been bullied into it?

Both looked at Sparky. He was a mess. He shivered and was terrified to the bone. Wolfy went to him and held him close. She looked over at Fate. She wanted to say thank you but had a huge lump in her throat. She let go of Sparky and sunk down to her knees and cried.

"Everyone wants to eat us, no one loves us," Wolfy whispered through her tears.

Fate stepped toward both of them. She put her protective wings over both of them. It was still raining.

Both rats were wet to the bone, but Fate was dry.

Q: Do you know why Fate was able to stay dry in the rain?

A rat's fur soaks up the water like your hair does when it's wet. Bird feathers repel water, and the drops roll off like pearls. That's how they stay dry, and some can even float on the water.

"This isn't so safe here," said Fate. "Why don't I bring you both up on the tree branch. We can talk and sort things out."

Both were unable to talk but nodded with their heads. Fate picked them up very carefully, one in each claw, and flew up to the tree branch. She set them down tenderly, sat between them, and put her wings over them to protect them from the ongoing rain.

Each was in their own solace. Fate wanted to give them comfort and hope but was in deep thoughts and sorrow herself. Why couldn't her family be more understanding and caring. Her own brother was so selfish and heartless.

Both rats were cuddled close to Fate, and she felt their comforting warmth on her body. Fate squeezed both gently closer to her and said to Wolfy, "You know, we all have days like this, where we lose our hope and trust. But remember, there's always a light at the end of the tunnel. After each dark night, there's a new day with light. Look at us three sitting here. We're giving each other hope for something new. Something no one ever thought could happen. Friendship between a rat and a bird of prey…enemies by nature. The force of nature brought us together and changed our path.

We're friends for life. We can't expect that everyone will change too but let this be a start."

Wolfy stopped crying, sniffled strongly, and said, "You're right, Fate. Thank you so much for saving Sparky's life. Now you don't owe me anything anymore. You are released from your promise...we're square. Your life for my brother's."

Fate looked at Wolfy and said, "I have a confession to make, Wolfy. When I saw you two down there and the snake approaching you, it crossed my mind just to turn a blind eye to the situation and all my problems would be solved. But that's not who I am and not someone I would like to become."

She smiled at Wolfy. Wolfy leaned silently into her rubbing gently at her feathers. Both looked at Sparky who hadn't said a peep since the whole incident.

"Is your brother a mute?" asked Fate.

Sparky looked from one to the other and shook his head and said, "I feel like a truck hit me, or I just woke up from a nightmare."

Fate said, "You both look a bit spooked. Wolfy has those red eyes from crying, and you look like a ghost. You both would be great for Halloween. Too bad that was last month!"

All three laughed loudly and felt relieved.

Wolfy said, "I guess it's safe to say your family will eat all of us except me, right?"

"Yup, very generous and kind of them, don't you think," said Fate sarcastically.

Q: What do you think about Fate's family decision? Do you think it is fair or not?

Wolfy then told Fate how it went with her family. "Well, my family kind of forgave me. Not all from my pack are happy about us. They don't trust our friendship."

Fate said, "My family didn't leave me lots of choices. I will leave tomorrow morning."

Without hesitation, Wolfy said, "I'm coming with you!"

Sparky swallowed hard and said, "You're leaving me, sis?"

"Yes, Sparky! I kind of got Fate into this situation. Besides, I always wanted to know what's out there, especially since I flew with Fate over the bay. Seeing so far, there's a whole lot more out there, Sparky. I will be back some day, I promise! We will sit up here on this branch, and I'll tell you all about it."

Fate was super excited and jumped from one foot to the other. Then she said, "There's only one problem."

Both rats looked at her. "What would that be?" Wolfy asked.

Fate asked, "Well how will you travel safely on my back?"

Sparky stepped forward and said, "I am a problem solver. I am an engineer! Let that be my thank you gift to both of you. Please, Fate, bring me down so I can start my project. I already have an idea. I once saw the *smelly* in a basket hanging underneath a hot-air balloon. I kept a little basket that might just fit your travel needs."

He had a huge smile and was excited to be of any use and help.

Wolfy smiled at Sparky and said, "Bring us both home, please. I've got to tell my family about leaving with you. It won't be easy, but I know my dad will understand."

Q: Do you know why?

Yes, because Wolfy's dad knows the excitement of adventure and travel.

Chapter 9

Something
Hard to Tell

The whole family was drawn into the story Sparky and Wolfy told them. They all took a sharp intake of air when told that Flo took Sparky into his claws.

"Oh nooo," said Rolfy, their dad. "You've got a powerful friend, Wolfy. I am proud of you. Your decision to help Fate that night has already paid forward. It saved your brother. I am looking forward to meeting your friend."

Wolfy and Sparky both looked a bit guilty.

"What is it? What are you not telling us?" Dad asked, looking worriedly from one to the other.

Wolfy murmured quietly through her teeth while leaning forward, "I am leaving with Fate."

"What! What are you saying?" Dad said, and he looked puzzled and hurt.

Wolfy's brother Porky repeated her words with his mouth full of food, "She said she's leaving with Fate," spitting half of his food everywhere.

"Yes, I heard that, Porky," Rolfy retorted.

Wolfy's mom stamped with her foot on the ground and held her paws onto her waist and said, "There's no way you can leave. We're your family. We're your home."

Wolfy turned toward her dad looking for support. He knew no matter how much this hurt him, he had to let her go. She was his daughter after all.

Q: Can you guess why?

Adventure was calling Wolfy. It was the same when Rolfy and Molly were young. Molly's parents didn't approve of him.

Rolfy put his paw around Molly, his wife, and squeezed her amicably and said, "My love, remember when your mom didn't want to let you marry me? Was there anything that could have stopped you from marrying me?"

She looked pensive at him. Her face changed from tense to playful sheepish.

The kids all knew what Mom would say because their parents tease each other all the time, and they all said together as if it were Mom talking, "Well, maybe a better-looking rat than you, Dad!"

The tension was broken and all united in good laughter, then Mom said, "You're right, Rolfy. She needs her turn to live her life too. All we can assure you, Wolfy, is that the door here will always be open for you."

In that moment, Charly stormed into the hole, his cheeks were blushed with excitement. He shouted, "It's the first rain everyone! Let's go to the Raindance Party!"

The Raindance Party is an old tradition in the animal kingdom of California and probably around the whole world. Since California has months of drought and only a couple of months of rain, the rain is treated sacredly by everyone in the animal kingdom. Hundreds of years ago, the animal kingdom had formed a treaty. The agreement between all animals was to come together from sunset till sunrise to celebrate the first rain of the year. The party would last all night long, and everyone was welcome.

Creatures of the day and night from the smallest to the largest, from the sky, from the ground, and from the underground were welcome to join.

No one was allowed to harm anyone else. It was a harmonious reunion because all understood that water was essential for all their lives. The need of water was something they all had in common.

Everyone looked puzzled at Charly, but it only took a split second to register the significance of this event. So many things had happened to them in the last few days, and they were all so busy. It didn't occur to them that the first rain had started.

It hit them all at once. "Perfect timing, Wolfy! We can celebrate all together and also make this your farewell party!" shouted Sparky.

Wolfy blushed with excitement and said, "Yes, and we can celebrate with my new friend Fate and meet her whole family."

Now it was Charly's turn to look puzzled, and he asked, "What farewell party, Wolfy? How long have I been gone?"

Chapter 10

Raindance Party

Rolfy looked around at everyone and took Charly by the paw. "Come, son, let's all go to the party, and we'll have plenty of time to fill you in."

Wild, excited chatter started, and everyone talked at once. When they surfaced on the football field, they were stunned how many animals had already arrived. Wild geese, ducks of all kinds, coyotes, cats, bobcats, skunks, owls, rabbits, turkeys, field mice, raccoons, opossums, hawks, snakes, foxes, owls, falcons, and many more. Fate's entire family was there too.

Q: Do you know some of these animals?

When Sparky saw Flo, he quickly hid behind his father's back and peeked out scared.

Flo winked with his eye at Sparky and said, "Hey, friend of my sister? How are you?"

Sparky retorted, "Thanks to *your* sister, I am still here tonight!"

"Now, now, let's be nice you two," said Fer, Flo's dad.

Rolfy stepped forward looking up at Fer and said, "You must be Fate's dad, our daughter's new friend."

Fer nodded with his head and replied, "I see, and you must be the father of the famous Wolfy."

Rolfy acknowledged proudly, "Yes indeed."

It was a madhouse for a moment. All talked with each other, laughed, and exchanged pleasantries. All felt the relief knowing that at last there was rain once again. Water was the essence of life, and they all wanted to live a bit longer. They were sitting peacefully in a large circle singing, dancing, talking, and dreaming of a better tomorrow.

They were all so busy that no one missed Sparky. He had gone back home to invent a safe traveling system for his sister and Fate. He had once seen the *smelly* in a basket hanging from a big hot-air balloon. This gave him a great idea.

Q: Have you ever seen a hot-air balloon? Did you ride on one?

A while ago Sparky had found a little basket made out of small wood splints, not knowing exactly what to do with it. Now he could visualize his sister sitting in it, flying with Fate high in the sky. He used some rubber bands and started to build something safe and useful for Wolfy and Fate.

Every now and then, he had to wipe a tear off his cheek knowing how much he would miss Wolfy.

There was someone else missing from the party unnoticed. It was Molly, Wolfy's Mom. She was busy at work on a pretty piece of fabric that Sparky had found and given to her a while ago. It was a bright hot-pink color. Sparky had told her secretly that Wolfy's dream was to own a dress; a pink dress to be precise. She never got around to it and now time was essential.

Molly's paws were fast at work. She made a little belt with a bow and used ruffled fabric from the waist down. She loved the look of it when she was finished. She even had some leftover fabric she used to make a matching ribbon for Wolfy's tail. She was really pleased with the outcome, and she tucked it inside a big walnut. It was their way of wrapping a present or to hide a gift.

In the meantime, Sparky finished his project too. He looked with great satisfaction at his creation that would serve as his sister's carriage. The color of the basket was brown. He found some plastic for the wall inside to help keep out water. He used some colorful felt over the plastic for comfort and as insulation. He tied a rubber band in a crisscross over the big opening and tied them with a big knot onto the side. It was meant for security and for Wolfy to hold on tight. Kind of like a seat belt for us in the car.

Q: Do you wear your seat belt?

It had a bowed handle also out of wood that was perfect for Fate to grab with her claws while taking off and to hold on during the flight. She would ride beneath Fate and would have Fate's protection from other predators in the air.

Sparky was pulling the basket behind him when he bumped into his Mom. Both had content and satisfied expressions on their faces.

Q: Can you guess why?

They both headed to the surface and back to the party. Mom with her walnut, and Sparky with his travel basket.

The party was in full swing when the two of them came back.

The circle dance had begun!

For this dance, two animals from different species dance together in the inner circle while all the others sit in a large circle around them, chanting and talking together. At the end of each dance, the two dancers were responsible to select two new animals who would then go into the inner circle to dance and so on until everyone had participated at least once.

Q: Do you know similar games from your birthday parties?

Everyone had a great time. You could hear excited howls, screeches, meows, deep and high growls, cackling, chatter, quacking, hooting, gaggling, grunting, purring, snarling, and squeaking hisses all at once.

Q: Can you make some of those sounds, and do you know who makes them?

Those animals knew how to throw a Raindance Party like no one else.

The usually grumpy rabbit was dancing with the foxy fox lady. He wasn't grumpy at all and was shaking his white cottontail to the left and right. The bushy tail from the fox was swirling like a helicopter blade around and brushed teasingly the rabbit's whiskers.

Mom spotted Wolfy first and pointed Sparky in her direction.

Wolfy was chatting up a storm with the great horned owl. She must have said something funny as the owl couldn't stop hooting. Mom reached Wolfy before Sparky. She tapped her on the shoulder and stepped to the side. Wolfy saw the Walnut and squeaked out a very loud cry of excitement.

Everyone stopped and looked surprised at Wolfy. She saw something sticking out of the Walnut and started pulling. Oh my goodness, could it be what she wished it was?

"A DRESS!" she squeaked even louder. "A PINK DRESS!"

"Put it on! Put it on!" everyone was chanting insistently.

She ran behind a metal board along the soccer field and changed into her dress. It fit perfectly and felt like a soft caress on her body. There was a water puddle in front of the metal sheet showing her reflection. It took her breath away. She turned around facing everyone. She heard the sounds of astonishment from all the animals. For the very first time, she felt like a girl. A beautiful *girl!*

She had her paws above her head and swirling around in a circle.

She said in a whisper and more to herself, "I am so beautiful!"

Her mom stepped closer and pulled out the ribbon and said, "Wait, my beautiful girl, I've got the best saved for last." She pulled out the pink ribbon and put it on her half tail.

Wolfy looked puzzled at her mom and said, "But, Mom, if I have a ribbon on my tail, everyone will see my half tail, and it would stand out!"

Mom said, "That's the point, Wolfy. Those who know you will be aware that this is the ribbon of a hero. And those who don't know you will ask how this happened. Wear your half tail with pride, not with shame. It will show everyone your perfect imperfection."

Q: Were you ever ashamed of something about yourself?

They all clapped with their paws or flapped their wings or rattled their tails chanting, "Dance for us!"

Rolfy started to yodel, and all animals pitched in with their own yodel sound. It sounded a bit scary but at the same time very powerful. At this point, it wasn't a secret anymore that Wolfy would leave with Fate in the morning.

Wolfy walked over to Fate, and she seemed to float over the grass.

Q: Did you ever get a gift or present that made you feel so good?

"Fate, would you do me the honor and dance with me?" asked Wolfy.

Fate had her own glow on her face. The awaiting adventure with Wolfy excited her tremendously. Fate said, "My pleasure, little princess."

Fate spread her wings and was moving them slowly back and forward. Her motion produced a soft breeze which pleasantly made Wolfy's dress waving in the wind. Wolfy almost had a glow around her…she was that pretty.

Sparky was waiting patiently on the outer circle for their dance to be over. After the dance, Fate chose one of the Geese who were living on the soccer field all year long. Wolfy picked a beautiful stalky bobcat for the next dance.

Sparky waved excitingly to Wolfy and Fate to come over. He adjusted his glasses because they had slipped down his nose out of excitement.

On the way there, Wolfy saw her Mom and stopped again to say, "Mom, I can't tell you how much this means to me. It's the most beautiful thing I have ever owned. Thank you so much, Mom!"

Her mom replied, "Your happiness is all the reward I was hoping for."

Wolfy asked, "How in the world did you know, Mom?"

Her mother nodded her head toward Sparky. She said with a big smile on her lips, "A little mouse whispered this in my ear."

Sparky looked at Mom and cried out whiny, "Mom!"

Wolfy went over to Sparky and kindly reminded him of something important.

"Remember, Sparky, Mom only teases those she loves." Wolfy gave him a big kiss, whispering in his ear, "I love you too, Sparky."

Sparky was embarrassed and deeply touched. He pressed her close and said, "I love you right back, sis."

"Come on you two," spat Sparky full of excitement to Fate and Wolfy. "I've got something very special for both of you!"

He held both paws together and gestured toward the basket and shouted, "Tadaaaaaaaa! Your very own travel basket!"

Wolfy and Fate both cried out, "Wow!" at the thrilling sight of the basket.

Wolfy turned around and flew into Sparky's arms at full speed with excitement and said, "It's magical, Sparky! It's such a magical night because of all of you!"

Sparky tried hard not to be knocked off-kilter when she threw herself into his paws with full swing. He struggled two steps backward trying to regain his balance. Wolfy was still in his arms when he lost it, and both fell over backward. Surprised by the moment, everyone got a good undiluted laughter.

Both dusted each other off, and luckily, Wolfy was on top of Sparky and not directly in the grass. Her dress was still spotless.

"Let's try it out, Fate," she said.

Chapter 11

Endings and Beginnings

Behind the hill over the Richardson Bay, you could see a slight glow of light. Sunrise was coming, and that would be the end of the Raindance Party and the treaty for this year.

Wolfy said, "I am so eager to try it out, Fate, but could you do my brother, the inventor, the honor of taking the first flight?"

Fate nodded her head in approval and said, "It will be my pleasure. Come on over, Sparky."

Sparky walked toward Fate, chest out, and he never looked taller when suddenly Flo stepped unexpectedly in front of Sparky, blocking him from reaching Fate. Sparky shuddered with fear and looked around worriedly.

Flo said, "It would be my honor to fly you, Sparky." He winked with his eyes fixed on Sparky and nudged him with his shoulder mischievously. "Just kidding, Sparky. It's the least I can do for my sister since I can't promise not to harm any of your pack…my heartfelt apology to you. I know I should stop teasing you. Maybe I'm a bit like your Mom. I only tease those I like."

Sparky shook his head and said, "Sorry, I would fly with you Flo, but it looks like you've lost some tail feathers which means you couldn't navigate, right?"

Bewildered, Flo swirled his head around only to see that all his feathers were there and all was fine. When he turned his head back to Sparky, he could see the big grin on Sparky's face. Everyone started to laugh at Flo.

Sparky said, "You're not the only one who starts to enjoy this, Flo."

Flo bent over and looked him in the eyes and said, "You got me good there. Peace for now, my friend?"

"How long will that be?" asked Sparky.

Flo grinned amiably at Sparky. "Well, let's start with this flight and then go from there. Shall we?" and he gestured for Sparky to climb into the basket.

Fate looked at Wolfy and said, "Looks like I am free for a flight with you after all. Just hold tight, and I'll be careful like the first time we flew together."

Fer stepped forward and looked at Rolfy and Molly and said, "My wife Fancy and I would love to take you two for a flight as well. This would be our way to show our thanks to your daughter for saving our daughter."

Rolfy looked very excited and Molly a bit scared. He took her by the paw and said, "This will be magical, Molly. Let's do it!"

All climbed up and took a safe place on the backs of the hawks, except for Sparky who was comfortable in the travel basket he had engineered. Almost on command, they swooshed up into the air. All the animals on the ground could hear their screeching for joy.

Q: Did you ever fly high up into the sky? Did you liked it or were you scared?

Slowly, the sun came up behind the mountain. All the animals made their last peace with everyone and said goodbye till next year.

In the meantime, the hawks took the rats over the Richardson Bay toward San Francisco. For a while, they couldn't stop the "ahhhs" and "oooohs." This was extraordinary for rats to get the experience of flying and the outlook which came with it. They could see so far, and everything underneath was so tiny and far below. This moment was all that mattered. They were flying close to each other and could point out at boats, towers, and the Golden Gate Bridge.

Rolfy shouted to Molly, "This is the bridge where my mom and I came over to Mill Valley. It changed my life because I met you there."

The whole flight took about thirty minutes and left everyone breathless; the rats from the sights and the hawks from the flight and the extra weight.

When they returned, the soccer field was empty, and everyone had left because at sunrise, the treaty had ended.

Q: Do you remember what that means?

Everyone got off the hawks' backs and had a bittersweet and somewhat gloomy smile on their faces. It had dawned on all of them that this also meant goodbye.

Rolfy looked around and thanked the parents of Fate for this unique adventure. Then he turned around looking at Wolfy and said, "Guess you're still leaving us, huh?"

"Yes, Dad," she said, looking solemnly at everyone. "I will miss you all terribly, especially you, Sparky, and my family." Tears poured out of her eyes and down her cheeks.

"At the same time, I'm excited to have this adventure with Fate. I know we will be back."

"Please promise me you will be back, Wolfy," Sparky said, looking at her through his tears.

"Yes, Sparky, I will have my pockets full of adventures to tell you all about," said Wolfy.

They hugged and kissed, and Wolfy said, "Dad, tell all my siblings goodbye and that I love them too. I don't have the strength to say goodbye to every single one."

Dad held her tight and promised to tell them.

At the same time, Fate had her goodbyes with her family.

Flo teased, "Sis, I can't believe you're leaving me for a rat." He winked at Fate and said, "Your friend is actually really cool. You taught me something important, and I will cherish this. Sorry, sis, that I can't pledge an oath."

"We all are sorry, Fate," said Fer.

Fate said, "I actually understand, and I don't hold it against you. I love you all!"

They moved close together and built a circle with their wings spread. It was their way to hug and wish farewell.

Wolfy left her beautiful new dress on and stuffed her old clothes into the travel basket and said, "For special times, Mom, you will always be close to my heart."

Her mom was so sad she couldn't speak but squeezed Wolfy close.

Wolfy climbed into the basket, and Fate grabbed the bow over the basket and took off.

Q: Do you know the sadness of goodbyes too?

Wolfy whispered, "Happy feathers and fur, Fate!"

"Happy feathers and fur to you too, Wolfy!" Fate replied.

"I guess I will be no longer nocturnal and will become like you, a diurnal critter. Let the journey begin," shouted Wolfy.

As they gained height, everyone got smaller and smaller. All were waving at each other until they were out of sight.

Fer, Fancy, and Flo said their goodbyes to Rolfy, Molly, and Sparky.

Flo nudged Sparky and winked at him saying, "I'll see you soon!"

Sparky answered, "Oh no you won't."

Both gave a last laugh and all went back home.

Up in the sky, Fate and Wolfy had decided to follow the coastline wherever it took them. Leaving Mill Valley, they flew along the bay toward the Golden Gate Bridge then turned with the coastline toward the ocean.

With the sun rising behind them, a new world of adventure opened up in front of them.

Q: Are you curious what adventures they will run into on their daily journey, not to mention the trouble they can get into together? Can you imagine?

Please write or e-mail me with your questions and your opinions because your voice matters to me.
WolfysAdventure123@gmail.com

Follow their adventure in the next book:

Here's a list of great places to bring or report an injured wild animal in California

At some of these places you can schedule an appointment to visit and learn about the injured animals and how you can prevent some of the injuries caused by nature or humans.

Everything below is publicly available information. If you live outside of Northern California, please Google and check out animal rescue places near you.

Please visit, volunteer, or donate to one of these wonderful places:

- Wilf Care in San Rafael
  Website: https://www.discoverwildcare.org
- Yggdrasil Urban Wildlife Rescue
  Website: http://yuwr.org
- Wildlife Care Association
  Website: https://wildlifecareassociation.com/found-animal/
- Fawn Rescue of Sonoma County
  Website: https://www.fawnrescue.org
- Gold Country Wildlife Rescue
  Website: https://goldcountrywildliferescue.org
- Suisun Marsh
  Website: http://www.suisunwildlife.org
- Lindsay Wildlife Rehabilitation Hospital
  Website: https://lindsaywildlife.org
- Lake Tahoe Wildlife
  Website: https://ltwc.org

- Tri County Wildlife Care
  Website: https://www.pawspartners.org
- Bird Rescue Center of Sonoma County
  Website: https://birdrescuecenter.org
- Wildlife Rescue Sonoma County
  Website: https://www.scwildliferescue.org
- Native Songbird Care & Conservation
  Website: http://nativesongbirdcare.org/Home.html
- Wildlife Center of Silicon Valley
  Website: https://wcsv.org
- Stanislaus Wildlife Care Center
  Website: http://stanislauswildlife.org
- Ohlone Humane Society Wildlife Rehabilitation Center
  Website: https://ohlonehumanesociety.org/wildlife-rehabilitation/
- Pacific Wildlife Care
  Website: https://www.pacificwildlifecare.org
- SPCA Wildlife Rescue & Rehabilitation Center
  Website: https://www.spcamc.org

About the Illustrator

Giulia McIsaac is originally from Davis, California, but has been living in San Francisco ever since she first started college. In the spring of 2020, Giulia graduated from the Academy of Art University with a BFA in animation and visual effects focusing in traditional animation. More of her work can be found on her website: giuliamcisaac.com.

When she is not working on an animation or illustration project, she can be found exploring new hiking trails in the Marin Headlands, running, beekeeping, or watching terrible movies with friends.

Giulia had a bunch of fun illustrating Wolfy and her friends for this adventurous story! She hopes you enjoy the story as much as she did!

About the Author

Gisela Bengfort-Piatti was born and raised in Switzerland where she met the love of her life, Joe Bengfort, in 1997. Six months later, they got married in the USA, and she moved with her two kids, Patrick and Selina, from Switzerland to the USA. They became a patchwork family as Joe also had two kids, Lindsey and Joseph.

Gisela frequently tells stories to their kids and grandkids about animals, empathy, making decisions, and unlimited possibilities.

Camryn, one of her grandkids inspired her to write down some of these family stories and true events from her past to the present.

Gisela loves the outdoors and all animals. You can find her on many Bay Area trails, sharing her laughter with family and friends.

While these stories are certainly fantasy, she has included many details about the animals that are factual including their behavior and their habitat. And just like with humans, animals can form unlikely relationships that bring unexpected joy and adventure.

Never stop to see the world through children's eyes unfiltered and untainted.

Use your imagination and enjoy the adventures of two animals becoming unlikely friends.

CPSIA information can be obtained
at www.ICGtesting.com
Printed in the USA
BVHW021216170622
640059BV00026B/938